way, side by side. This is a story of how one king came
to be king of all the rest. And it all began with a
dream in a pigsty.

An exciting story of Norway in the early days,
retold from an old Norse hero tale.

THE DREAM
OF KING ALFDAN

AN OLD NORSE HERO TALE

Retold by Isabel Wyatt

ILLUSTRATIONS BY EVERETT KINTSLER

Follett Publishing Company

Chicago

© 1961, by Isabel Wyatt
Manufactured in the United States of America
Published simultaneously in Canada by
The Ryerson Press

Library of Congress Catalog Card Number: 61-8803

123456789

THE DREAM OF KING ALFDAN

1: How Haki Was Made a Wolf's Head

King Sigurd the Hart was king of Ring-Rik in Norway. At the birth of his son he held a splendid feast.

At the feast, King Sigurd sat in his high seat, and the newborn prince was laid at his feet. And King Sigurd gave the boy the name of Guthorm.

To this birth-feast came the two kings of the two lands next to Ring-Rik. They sat next to King Sigurd, at the top of the long table that ran the length of the long hall.

Next to the kings sat lords, in red furs and gold arm rings. And next to the lords sat the men, in coats of mail.

The lords drank deep of wine from golden wine cups. The men drank deep of ale, from ale horns bound with silver. And the king's hall rang with songs and jests and mirth.

Soon men who had drunk too deep began to sprawl and to brawl. They began to shout and to brag, and to pluck at dagger and sword hilt.

Ragnild, the new prince's sister, came in, to bring the king's wine in a guest-cup. She was only six years old. But even then she had the by-name of Ragnild the Golden, so gay a gold was her hair.

She gave the guest-cup first to the king next to her father. This was the young King Alfdan the Black. As he drank from it, she threw back her head to gaze at his black hair.

"Never did I see black hair till now," she said. "In Ring-Rik our hair is golden."

"Ah," said King Alfdan the Black, "but I have a golden

roof, the only one in all Norway. My hall is by a lake; and in the sun you can see its roof flash like gold fire over the water."

"My father's grave mound will be by a lake," said the small princess. "A wise man told him that it must be by a lake, that it might help me in my hour of need."

King Alfdan gave her back the guest-cup. She gave it to the next king, King Eric the Merry. King Eric had red hair. His eyes were full of fun.

"What roofs do kings with red hair have?" asked the small princess.

"Roofs of straw, that birds can nest in," King Eric told her. "And the birds sing, to tell the kings with red hair things that will come to pass."

King Eric spoke in jest. Yet what he said was true. For he had the sight that can see a man's fate. And it was when the birds sang in his hall thatch that his gift came upon him.

"What do the birds sing about King Alfdan?" asked the small princess.

"They sing," said King Eric, "that he will dream a dream in a pigsty. The dream will only be a dream about his own hair. Yet with that dream will be bound up a new fate for all Norway."

"What do the birds sing about me?" asked the small princess.

"They sing," said King Eric, "that you will help to make that dream in the pigsty come true."

"What do the birds sing about you?" asked the small princess.

"They sing," said Eric, "that I, and this newborn Prince Guthorm, and that small boy who peeps in at the door, will all help to make the dream in the pigsty come true."

The small princess swept round to look at the boy at the door.

"That is Koll," she said. "He is my playmate. The lord next to you is his father. And the lord next to him is the father of those two big boys with Koll. They are Arek and Askel; they are my playmates, too. Will they help the dream in the pigsty to come true?"

"The birds did not say so," said King Eric, "so I do not think they will."

Koll's father shook the arm of the father of Arek and Askel. On his face was the flush of too much wine.

"Hear you that, Haki?" he cried. "My son will play a part in Norway's fate. But your sons will not."

"Say you so?" cried Haki, red with rage.

And in a flash his sword was out and had struck Koll's father a deathblow.

A hush fell then on all the hall. All eyes were on King Sigurd.

With a deep sigh, King Sigurd rose from his high seat.

9

"Haki," he said, "in one flash of rage you rob me of two good lords. For you know the law. For that thrust I must make you a wolf's head."

The small Princess Ragnild asked low of King Eric: "What is a wolf's head?"

King Eric bent and spoke into her ear:

"An outlaw. He must give up his hall and his lands and all that is his. He has three days of grace; then all who see him will be free to slay him."

"Poor Haki!" said Ragnild the Golden. "Then what can he do?"

"All he can do," said King Eric, "is to flee from the parts of the land that men dwell in. He must find a place to dwell in in some wild part where men do not go."

And this was what Haki the Wolf's Head did.

When Haki fled, the small Princess Ragnild lost two of her playmates. For with Haki went his wife, and his men, and his two young sons.

To a wild part of Ring-Rik they rode, a part too wild for most men to dwell in. It was full of crags and cliffs; no green was to be seen.

In it they came to a wide cleft in the cliffs. From the foot of the steep cliffs, far, far below, came the rush and roar of swift water.

"On the far side of such a cleft," said Haki the Wolf's Head, "even a wolf's head will be safe."

It was too wide a gap for a man to leap on foot. But it was not too wide for a good steed. So over the cleft, from cliff top to cliff top, one by one, sprang Haki's band on Haki's steeds.

Then on they rode, till they came to a thick fir wood. And on among the fir trees they rode, till they came to a vast lake deep in the wood.

"In this wood will we dwell," said Haki the Wolf's Head. "On this side the lake will guard us, and on that side the steep cleft."

"Father," said Arek, "let us set a trip cord on our side of the cleft. Then if a steed springs over, the cord will jolt it as it lands. And that will cast its rider over the cliff into the river far below."

"No man who has no need to will seek to cross such a cleft," said Haki. "All the same, my son, a trip cord we will set. And it shall be yours, Arek, to look after."

So a trip cord was set. And each day Arek went to see that it had not been sprung.

Soon Haki the Wolf's Head had a new hall, hidden deep in the fir wood. It was not as fine a hall as his old one; but it had a bower for his wife, and the bower had an inner room for her two young sons.

When Arek and Askel grew older, they left this inner room and went to sleep in the sleeping-room of the men. Then Haki's wife took the inner room to dry her herbs. For this she had need of a stream of air; so the men made her a round hole high in the wall. The Norse name for such an air hole in the old days was a "wind's eye."

Haki's wife used the herbs to heal the sick, for she was the leech in that hall of outlaws. When one of Haki's men was sick or hurt, he came to her to heal him. She had much skill in such things, as a lord's wife had in those days.

12

Arek was much with his father; but Askel was much with his mother. She saw, as he grew, that Askel had a love of herbs. So she took care to teach her skill to him, that he might take her place as leech to the outlaws when her time came to die.

From time to time, Haki and his outlaws went over the cleft by night. To the rich parts of Ring-Rik they rode, to rob and to raid. So they soon had good store of gold and of gear. Yet with such craft and skill did they make their raids that no man was able to track them back to the hall in the fir wood.

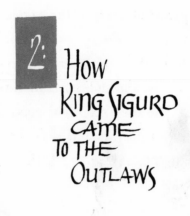

2: How King Sigurd Came To The Outlaws

So ten years went by. Haki's wife died. Arek and Askel began to grow up. In all that time, no boat came over the lake. In all that time, no steed sprang over the cleft. In all that time, no man in all Ring-Rik found Haki's hall in the wilds.

So ten years went by. Then, one day at the end of the fall, King Sigurd rode out alone to hunt the stag.

Such joy did he take in this that from it he had got his by-name of Sigurd the Hart.

He had not ridden far when a tall stag ran by. And off he set to hunt it.

Swift was the speed of the stag. Swift was the speed of King Sigurd's steed. Over hill and dale sped the stag. Over hill and dale sped King Sigurd after it.

By dusk the stag had led him into a part of his land he did not know. All about him were vast crags and steep cliffs; no green was to be seen.

The stag came to a wide, deep cleft in the cliffs. From the foot of the cliffs, far, far below, came the rush and roar of swift water.

Over the cleft, from cliff top to cliff top, sprang the stag.

Over the cleft, from cliff top to cliff top, sprang King Sigurd on his steed.

Across the far cliff top a trip cord ran. The stag sprang clear of it. But King Sigurd's steed sprang into it. So sudden and sharp was the jolt that the king was thrown.

His head hit the crag as he fell. Over that steep cleft he hung, his left foot still held in its stirrup.

Still lay the king. Still stood the steed. Still were crag and cliff in the dusk all about them.

Then, with slow steps, the steed began to drag the king away from the cleft. Its hoof took the trip cord with it.

On went the steed, till it came to a thick fir wood.

Into this wood it went.

By now it was dark. Soon the full moon came up. Still on in the moonlit dark went the steed, deep into the wood.

Deep in the wood, hidden among the thick fir trees, the steed came to a hall.

15

At the door of the hall the steed came to a halt.

The door of the hall was shut. On it, with its hard front hoof, the steed gave three raps, loud and sharp.

Haki the Wolf's Head and his outlaws sat at meat in the hall. Pine brands lit along the walls cast a red glow on silver dish and golden wine cup, the spoil of the outlaws' raids.

At the sound of those three raps, the men sat stiff and still, ale horn in hand. The gaze of all went to the door.

"Our first guest in all our ten years here!" cried Haki. "Ten men to the door, and let us see this night guest!"

The ten men next to the door rose from the table. They went to the door and slid back the bar that held it fast. All ten stood sword in hand as the door swung gently open.

From moonlit night to torchlit hall, with slow steps, King Sigurd's steed came in. By the left foot still held in the stirrup, it drew the prone king after it.

Up sprang the men from the table. But Haki cried down the hall:

"Each man stay in his place! Let Askel first tend this man!"

Askel knelt by the king. He felt the king's head, his wrist, his brow. He laid his ear to the king's chest and to the king's lips.

Then he stood up.

"Father," he said, "this man is not yet dead. But so sore are his hurts that in three days he will be. It seems that he fell from his steed and broke his skull in the fall."

"That must have been at the cleft," said Arek, "for I see my trip cord on the steed's hoof."

"But why came he to the cleft?" asked Haki. "I do not think it was to seek us out, for it is long since our last raid."

"It may be that a stag led him," said Askel, "for he is clad for the hunt. And yet he can be no simple hunter. He has the look of a man of good birth."

At this, Haki rose and came down the hall. He bent low over the king. In the dim red glow, it was hard to see him plain.

"Bring me a torch!" cried Haki.

Arek ran to him with a lit pine brand. He held it to the king's face.

"A man of good birth he is," said Haki. "I know this face well, even after ten years. For I was his man till he made me a wolf's head. This is King Sigurd the Hart!"

From lip to lip flew the name. All down the long bench a hubbub broke out:

"If he is so near his death hour, who will rule Ring-Rik next? For Prince Guthorm is but ten years old."

"Ragnild the Golden is sixteen. She is of age to rule."

"But king's men look to be led by a king."

"Well, is she not of age to wed? The man who weds her will be king."

"Some man will have luck, then."

"Why not our Lord Haki?"

At that, one and all took up the cry:

"Let Lord Haki wed Ragnild the Golden! And let us all be king's men!"

Haki the Wolf's Head held up his hand. A hush fell.

18

"First things first," said Haki. "Askel, take four men and bear the king to a bed. Tend his hurts, and stay at his side."

Four men rose from the bench and came to King Sigurd. They took him up and bore him from the hall. Askel the Leech went with them.

Then, with bent head, Haki trod the length of his hall, to and fro, to and fro. To and fro, to and fro, the eyes of his men went with him. In that long hall, the only sound was the tramp of Haki's feet.

Then he stood still. He threw up his head.

"This plan you din in my ears is a bold plan, men!" he cried. "We shall need to think it out well. But we will try it!"

Back on his high seat, chin in hand, Haki made his plans, with Arek at his side to help him.

"The king's men will have no fear for the king as yet," said Haki. "For I call to mind that it has ever been his way, if the hunt took him far, to spend the night in the open."

"And *I* call to mind," said Arek, "that when he did this, it was ever Ragnild's way to ride out alone next dawn to meet him."

"Then she plays into our hands," cried Haki. "For we can whisk her away as she rides out at dawn and be back for the bride feast by sunset."

"We must take Prince Guthorm, too," said Arek, "lest,

19

with the princess lost, the king's men make him king."

"When King Sigurd dies," said Haki, "the king's men will not know it. The first they will know of it will be when Queen Ragnild rides into her hall, with King Haki at her side. So we do not need to take Prince Guthorm, if he is not with her. If he is with her, it will be best to take him too."

"Will you bring her by force, or coax her, or hoax her?" asked Arek.

"We will give her the true news that the king lies nigh to death," said Haki. "I think that then she will come of her own free will. Now Askel shall stay to tend the king, and a third of the men to deck the hall for the bride feast. Bid the rest bring out the steeds. We must be on our way in an hour if we are to meet my bride at dawn!"

3: How the Outlaws Took Ragnild the Golden

At dawn the next day, Ragnild the Golden rode out from the king's hall to meet her father. She had grown tall and fair of face, and her hair was still as gay a gold as when she was a child.

"I will ride with you, sister," said the small Prince Guthorm. "For you need a man to guard you, now you are of age to wed."

Koll, Princess Ragnild's old playmate, was now King Sigurd's page.

"A ten-year-old shrimp of a lad is no guard for a golden princess," said Koll. "I think I had better come too, and guard you both."

So off all three set in the dawn.

Out they rode among the fields that had been full of

ripe red corn a few weeks ago. On they rode, across the green vale that fed the cows. And so they came into a bright wood of silver birch trees.

As they rode in the wood, Ragnild the Golden held back her steed.

"Do you hear hoofbeats?" she asked.

Thud, thud, thud, came the beat of hoofs from far away.

"I know that hoofbeat," said the small Prince Guthorm. "It is our father's steed. How fast he rides home today!"

Thud, thud, thud, came the hoofbeats, loud and louder, near and nearer. Then into sight, among the silver birch trees, came a steed.

"Yes," said Ragnild the Golden, "that is our father's steed. But is that our father on it?"

"It is not," said Koll. "It is someone I have never seen. And yet it seems to me that it is someone I did see, long ago."

As the rider came near to them, he drew his steed up sharp.

"Princess Ragnild!" he cried. "I come to you from King Sigurd the Hart. You will know this steed for his. And he sends you his ring."

He held out a ring to her.

"What ails my father?" cried Ragnild. "Yes, yes, this is his steed, and this his ring."

"He fell from his steed and is sore hurt," said the rider. "He lies now at my hall. I come to take you to him."

"Koll," said the princess, "ride back and fetch men to bear my father home. My brother and I will ride on with you, my lord. How is it that I do not know your face or name?"

Koll bent his brows as he swung around his steed to ride back to the hall. He felt he knew that man. And he felt he did not trust him.

And then it came to him who it was. He knew that face from when he was a child, ten years ago. He knew it for the face of the man who had slain his father.

"It is Haki the Wolf's Head!" he cried.

And he flung his dagger at Haki. It cleft Haki's mail. It went deep into his side.

Then from among the birch trees came steed after steed, each with its rider clad in mail, spear in hand and sword at side. Amid that sudden throng of men, the prince and princess did not see the spear flung after Koll. They did not see Koll fall.

One rider cried, as he rode to Haki's side:

"Father, are you hurt?"

"I can last till Askel can tend me, Arek," said Haki.

"Arek!" cried Ragnild the Golden. "If this is true that your father tells me of my father, why is it with spears that you come to fetch me to him?"

"What my father tells you is true, Princess Ragnild," said Arek. "It is only with spears that we *can* come; for call to mind that we are outlaws. All men are free to slay us at sight, as you saw Koll seek to slay my father. Each of us risks his life, Princess, to bring you to the king."

Ragnild the Golden bit her lip and bent her head, for she saw that this was true.

"You are right," she said. "And much do I owe you all. Now let us ride to my father."

At a swift pace the throng of men set off, with the prince and princess in the midst of them. By secret by-ways they cut across the land to the wild, bare tract of crags and cliffs. They did not stop till they came to the wide, deep cleft, with its rush and roar of swift water far below.

"It was at this cleft that the king your father fell, Princess," said Arek. "Shall I bind you to your steed for the leap across?"

"No," said Ragnild the Golden. "I can sit my steed."

"Shall I bind *you* to your steed, Prince?" asked Arek.

"No," said the small Prince Guthorm. "I can sit my steed."

"Bind me, my son," said Haki, with a gasp. "For I am weak from loss of blood."

Arek bound his father to King Sigurd's steed. Over the wide cleft, from cliff top to cliff top, one by one, sprang the steeds.

"Do not unbind me, Arek, lest I fall," said Haki, his hand to his side. "Set up the trip cord when the last steed is over."

This Arek did. Then on and into the fir wood they rode. And so they came to Haki's hidden hall.

Cries and shouts of joy met them at the door of the hall. But the joy was cut short when the men who ran out saw Haki droop on his steed.

So weak was he now that his men had to lift him down and bear him into the hall.

"Bear me to my bed, men," said Haki. "Arek, bring our guests to the king. And send Askel to me. Tell him I have need of his skill."

Prince Guthorm's eyes were wide as he was led into the hall. For its long table was set with gold and silver, as if for a feast, and a blaze of cloth-of-gold lay on the long bench and on the high seat.

Across fresh straw Arek led the prince and princess to his mother's bower.

"It was my mother's way, when one of us was sick," he told them, "to tend him in her bower. So it is in her bower, that is now *your* bower, Princess, that we have laid the king."

As they came into the bower, Askel the Leech rose from his seat by the king's bed. Ragnild the Golden ran to meet him.

25

"Askel, how is my father?" she cried.

Askel bent low over her hands.

"Princess, he sleeps. He can last but a short time now," he said.

Ragnild laid her hand on her father's brow, then sank into Askel's seat. Here she sat, as still as the still form on the bed, till Arek came in with a silver bowl of water.

He knelt to wash the hands and feet of his guests, as was the way in the old days.

"That chest holds all my mother's gear, Princess," he said. "Take from it what you need. This inner room is yours, Prince. It was mine and Askel's when we were boys, and the chest in it is full of our gear from when we too were ten years old. Take what you need."

"My father's end is not far off," said Ragnild the Golden. "So set no place for me in the hall, Arek; I will stay with him till the end."

"You shall do as you will, Princess," said Arek.

And to himself he said, "Since the bride feast must be put off."

For as soon as Askel had seen the gash in Haki's side, he had told him:

"Father, with this gash in your side you will hold no bride feast this night, nor for many nights to come."

"No matter, so I hold it in the end," said Haki. "Koll has put off the bride feast. But I still hold Ring-Rik's new queen."

4: HOW PRINCESS RAGNILD SAW THE GOLDEN ROOF

That night, as the princess sat at his side, King Sigurd the Hart died in his sleep. Ragnild the Golden wept over him. Then she took the king's ring and set it on the small Prince Guthorm's thumb.

"For you are king of Ring-Rik now, little brother," she told him.

But Prince Guthorm drew the big ring from his thumb and gave it back to her.

"Wear it for me, Ragnild," he said. "I am too small yet to be a king. Koll calls me just a ten-year-old shrimp of a lad, and Koll is right."

"What ails Koll, that he takes so long to bring our father's men?" asked Ragnild. "We have need of them now to seek a lake, and to make our father's grave mound at its side."

But when she said this to Arek, he told her:

"Princess, a lake lies but a stone's cast from this hall. Our men will make the king's grave mound at its side for you."

"Take me to this lake," said Ragnild the Golden, "that I may find the right place for my father's bones to lie."

"Then come with me now," said Arek. "At this dawn hour our men go to the lake to draw water."

So out into the dawn went the princess and the small prince, with Arek and the men with the water butts. Two and two they went along the track among the fir trees, the track that led away from the cleft.

Soon they came to the end of the track. To the left stood the wild, thick wood. To the right stood the wild, thick wood. And in front lay a lake so vast that it was water, water, water, all the way to the far sky.

Along the bank the men spread out, to fill the water butts. To and fro at the lakeside went Ragnild the Golden with slow steps and bent head, till she knew she had found the place for her father's grave mound.

"Let it be here," said she.

So in Ragnild's bower, King Sigurd the Hart lay in state. And at the lakeside, Haki's men cut down fir trees and made a round room in the ground for King Sigurd the

Hart to sit in, with gold and gear, and with sword and shield, and with all that a king in the old days took with him into his grave.

And still Koll and the king's men did not come to the hall in the wilds. So it was Haki's men who set King Sigurd the Hart in the round room, and over it made a mound, wide and high, to mark the grave of a king.

Then said Ragnild the Golden to Arek:

"Now that my father is laid to rest, I must go back to his hall with my brother, that he may be made king. And his first act as king shall be to give back to Lord Haki his lands, and to give all in this hall free pardon."

But Arek said:

"Princess, it is not my father's will that your brother be made king. He wills that you be queen. And he wills that you stay here till he is well. And then he wills to wed you."

"Haki wills to wed me?" cried Ragnild the Golden. "Has Koll's dagger sent him mad?"

She swung round in rage, and swept into her bower, and shut the door with a bang.

Out from the inner room came the small Prince Guthorm. He came with a slip and a slide, for he had boy's skates on his feet.

"Look, Ragnild!" he cried. "I found skates that fit me in Arek's chest. They must have been his when he was my age. Why, Ragnild! Why are you in such a rage?"

Then Ragnild sank into a seat and drew him to her, and told him all that Arek had said.

As he sat and took off the skates, Guthorm said:

"I think this plot must have been in Haki's mind from the first; for as we came into the hall, I saw that it was laid for a feast. I think it would have been your bride feast, Ragnild, had not Koll's dagger put it off."

"How can Haki dream he can make me wed him," cried Ragnild, "when he knows Koll is on his way to us with a band of our father's men?"

"But is Koll on the way?" asked Prince Guthorm. "If this plot was in Haki's mind from the first, then he left no men in the birch wood, to guide our men to this hall. If this plot was then in Haki's mind, it may be that he had Koll slain, so that now our own men have no clue as to what befell us."

"If what King Eric said at your birth feast was true," said Ragnild, "Koll cannot be slain. For Koll was to help to make the dream in the pigsty come true."

"It is Koll who has put off the bride feast," said Guthorm. "It may be that that was his help. Our men must have ridden far and wide by now to seek us, Ragnild, but I think this hall is too well hidden for them ever to find it. Shall we not try to slip out and find our own way back?"

"The door of my bower is our only way out," said

31

Ragnild. "Go, Guthorm, and try that door. I fear you will find that a bar has been set across it."

The small prince set down the skates and ran to try the door. A bar on the far side held it fast.

"You are right, Ragnild," he said. "This way we cannot go. But my room has a wind's eye. If we can get up to it, we can slip out by that."

"We can, if you have a spell to make me as small as you, little brother," said Ragnild with a sad smile. "For I am far too big as I am to slip out of a wind's eye."

"Then I will go," said Guthorm, "and bring our men back to free you."

"And will you fly across the cleft to fetch them?" asked Ragnild, with her sad smile.

"No, I will steal a steed from the stable," said the small prince.

"First you must put the stablemen to sleep," said Ragnild.

Then said the small Prince Guthorm:

"Since we can find no way to cross that cleft, we must try the other way."

"And how will you cross the lake?" asked Ragnild. "I saw no boat by the bank. Will you grow wings?"

A flick of Prince Guthorm's hand swept aside the skates, and they fell with a clang.

"Why, Ragnild!" he cried. "It is the end of the fall.

In a week or two we shall see ice on the lake. Then I shall not need boat or wings; I can cross on Arek's skates!"

Ragnild the Golden bent and gave him a hug.

"Ah, if we did but know what is on the far side!" she said with a sigh. "It may well be a wild land, as this is, too wild for good men to dwell in."

Prince Guthorm sat at her feet, his small chin in his small hand. He was still for a time.

"Ragnild," he said at last, "tell me again what the wise man told our father about his grave mound."

"He told him," said Ragnild, "that it must be at the side of a lake, that it might help me in my hour of need."

"Then seek its help," said the small prince. "For it seems to me that this is your hour of need."

When it was time to eat, the door of the bower swung open and men came in with rich food in a golden dish and with wine in golden wine cups.

As Princess Ragnild took the food, she said to them:

"Tell Lord Arek it is my wish, when next you go to draw water, to go with you to my father's grave to pray."

"We will tell him, Princess," said the men.

So again the prince and the princess went out into the wood with Arek and the men with the water butts. Two and two they went along the track among the fir trees. But with them this time, in front and at the back, went men with spears.

When they came to the lake, the men spread along the bank to draw water.

"I will go to the top of the mound alone," said Princess Ragnild. "My brother will stay here with you, below."

The men with the spears spread to stand round the foot of the mound. With slow steps and bent head, Ragnild the Golden went up its slope. She came to the crest, and

sat down to look about her. It was as if she sat on the top of a small hill.

She let her mind grow still, that if any help came, she might hear it. As she sat, looking on the water, the sun came out. And far away in front of her, she saw a flash of gold.

"What can that be?" she asked herself. "It came like a flash of gold fire over the water."

And then her mind went back ten years. She saw her father's hall at the newborn Guthorm's birth feast. She saw herself, a small princess six years old, come in with the golden guest-cup. She saw herself give the guest-cup to a king with black hair.

"Never did I see black hair till now," said that small princess. "In Ring-Rik our hair is golden."

And what was it that the king with the black hair had said back to her?

Her eyes grew bright as it all came back:

"Ah, but I have a golden roof, the only one in all Norway. My hall is by a lake; and in the sun you can see its roof flash like gold fire over the water."

So now she knew that King Alfdan of Hadland had his hall on the far side of the lake. It came to her then that the outlaws did not know this. It came to her that what she had seen was a secret. She saw that to see that flash you had to be high in the air, as she was on the crest of her father's grave mound. Down below, on the bank, that gold fire did not show.

When Ragnild and Guthorm were in her bower again, Guthorm asked:

"Did our father's grave mound help in your hour of need, Ragnild?"

"It did, little brother," she told him. "I know now that all will yet be well with us. For on the far side of the lake dwells the king who is to dream the dream in the pigsty."

5: How Prince Guthorm Went For Help

Each night after that, when the prince and the princess were left alone and the bar held the bower door fast, they swept the straw from part of the floor. Then, in the dust, Ragnild the Golden drew a map of the sky, to teach the small prince how to find his way across the lake with the help of the stars.

Each day the prince and the princess went to the lake with the men who went to draw water. When Ragnild had sent to say that this was her wish, Askel the Leech had said to Haki:

"It is good to let them do this, Father. For at the king's hall the princess was much out-of-doors; if she lacks fresh air now, she may well fall sick. With Arek and the men about them, they cannot slip away."

Day by day the cold grew, till the day came when they went out to find snow in deep drifts on the track. And soon after this came the day when they stood on the bank of the lake and saw in front of them one vast sheet of ice.

That day Arek said, as they went back:

"In three days, Askel tells me, our father can rise from his bed and hold his bride feast. In three days, Princess, you will be my stepmother, and you, Prince, my small uncle!"

As soon as they were alone for the night, Ragnild the Golden said:

"It must be soon now, Guthorm, or we shall be too late."

"Let it be now," said the small prince. "It is full moon, and that will be all to the good."

He took Arek's skates from the chest, and set thick furs about him. Ragnild gave him a kiss. She gave him a hug.

They set a bench by the wall of the inner room, so that it stood under the wind's eye. They stood on the bench; into her arms Ragnild took him, to lift him to the wind's eye.

As she held him up, he was just able to stretch and reach to the high round hole. He was just able to cling and to hang from it by his hands.

"May Ull, the god of snowshoes, be with you, little brother," said Ragnild the Golden.

Prince Guthorm drew his small form up to the wind's eye. He got out one foot to the far side. He got out both feet to the far side. Out he went. Over he went. He hung and clung by his hands in the sharp night air.

Moss grew on the outer wall of the hall. Grass grew on the outer wall of the hall. So it was not hard for Guthorm to find footholds. It was not hard for him to find handholds.

Inch by inch down the wall slid the small prince, till his foot felt the soft snow on the ground.

Into the moonlit fir wood he stole. The footprints left by the men that day were black in the white snow. Along the track they led him, among the fir trees, to the lake.

He stood on the bank of the lake, at the foot of his father's grave mound, and he drew in a deep, deep breath.

To the left he saw a long, long plain of ice stretch away, away, away, to melt into the far dark.

To the right he saw a long, long plain of ice stretch away, away, away, to melt into the far dark.

In front he saw a long, long plain of ice stretch away, away, away, to melt into the far dark.

He bent, and bound his skates to his feet.

Up he stood, and drew his furs about him. Then, as light as a bird, and as swift as a bird, he began to skim across that moonlit, misty, vast white plain of ice.

So fast he flew that his swift flight made a wind. Chill, chill, chill, blew that wind. Even with Arek's furs about him, Guthorm felt that chill creep into his bones.

So fast he flew, and so vast was the plain he flew over, that it began to seem as if it was in a dream that he flew. The white light of the moon, the white mist, the white ice, all were like something in a dream.

So clear were the stars that he was able to match them with the map of the sky he had laid up in his mind, night by night. He was able to steer his track by them.

So bright a light did the full moon give that after a time he was able to make out dim forms along the sky line, far in front of him. On he flew; he saw now that the dim, dark forms were trees.

Still on he flew. The trees drew near; the trees grew clear.

At last, in the long dark line of trees, he saw a gap. And in the gap he saw the light of the moon gleam on a roof, part white with snow, part bright with gold, that was set among the trees.

And such was his joy that he sang out loud:

"I have come across the lake from Ring-Rik to Hadland! I have found the hall with the golden roof of King Alfdan the Black!"

He drew in to the bank. Stiff and sore, he came up off the ice on to the snow. He unbound his skates. Up the slope he went, and under the porch to the door of King Alfdan's hall.

He felt for the guest horn that hung at the side of the door. He set it to his lips. He blew a blast on it.

The door swung wide. In from the moonlit night, with slow, stiff steps, went a small lad clad in furs, a pair of skates in his hand.

A hush fell on the men about the fires as the lad went up the hall and stood in front of the high seat. On

the high seat sat King Alfdan. So black was his hair that
the lad threw back his head to gaze at it.

"Never did I see black hair till now," he said. "In
Ring-Rik our hair is golden."

"A small princess said the same to me ten years ago,"
said King Alfdan.

"That was at my birth feast," said the small prince.
"I am Prince Guthorm of Ring-Rik. My father, King Sigurd
the Hart, is dead. Haki the Wolf's Head holds my sister.
In three days he wills to wed her, that he may take the
land for his own."

"You sway on your feet, Prince," said King Alfdan.
"Sit, eat, and drink. Then tell me all your tale."

Stiff and sore, the small prince sat. He ate. He drank.
He told the king all his tale. Then he went to sleep with
his head in the dish.

Said Torlef, King Alfdan's wise man:

"Let him sleep, lord. A grown man might well be
worn out by what this lad has made his small self do this
night."

King Alfdan cried down the hall:

"Let each man bring out his sledge, to cross the
lake to Ring-Rik."

The small prince still slept as Torlef took him up and
bore him out to the king's sledge.

"Let him sleep, lord," he said again. "We have no

need of him yet. The marks of his skates on the ice will guide us over the lake."

And in Torlef's arms the small prince still slept as the sledge sped over the vast plain of ice, with three of King Alfdan's strong steeds to pull it, as swift as black birds in the moonlight.

Not till the sledge drew up by King Sigurd's grave mound on the far bank of the lake did Torlef the Wise wake the lad.

"We need your help now, Prince Guthorm," he told him. "Show us the way to Haki's hall."

They left a small band of men with the steeds. The rest the small prince led along the track among the fir trees.

All was still in Haki's hall. Deep sleep held the outlaws as King Alfdan broke in.

Short and sharp was the fight. To left and to right the outlaws fell, as the small prince led Torlef the Wise to the door of the bower, and slid back the bar.

"Ragnild! Ragnild!" he cried.

Then he was with her. Her arms were about him. Her gay gold hair was about him.

With Torlef he led her out into the free air of the moonlit night. He ran with her along the track to the lake. He set her in the king's sledge.

Then King Alfdan came back to his sledge. Back to their sledges came King Alfdan's men.

Then up from his sickbed rose Haki the Wolf's Head. He took up his sword.

Out to the stable he crept. He found King Sigurd's steed. Down to the edge of the lake he rode, asway in his saddle, his sword asway in his hand.

They saw him loom, black in the moonlight. They saw the steed slip as it set a hoof on the ice. They saw Haki thrown from his saddle, as Sigurd the Hart had been thrown. They saw Haki fall on his sword at the foot of King Sigurd's grave mound.

He knew then that his death hour was upon him.

"You have won my princess from me, Alfdan the Black," he cried. "But when you reach the age that I am now, take heed. Take heed, lest ice bring you to your death then, as now it brings me to mine."

And with that he died.

"Lord," said Torlef the Wise to King Alfdan, "let us take this wolf's head with us, and give him a hero's grave. Thus you may get free from his death wish."

So they took up Haki and set him in the sledge.

"How old was Haki, Guthorm?" asked King Alfdan.

"Forty years old," the small prince told him.

"Ah, then," cried King Alfdan, gay of mood, "I have twice seven years to live till I need fear this ice fate!"

Then back across the lake they went to the hall with the golden roof.

6: THE QUEEN'S DREAM AND THE KING'S DREAM

When he got back to Hadland, King Alfdan the Black gave Haki the Wolf's Head a hero's grave.

A round room was dug for him at the lakeside, south of the hall with the golden roof, by the Place of the Cattle Branding. A mound was made over it, to mark the grave of a hero.

The day after the flight across the ice, King Alfdan the Black got up at dawn to greet the sun.

When he went to go out by the sunrise door of his hall, he found the bar drawn back. And when he went out, a golden princess stood by the wall, to greet the sun with him.

Then King Alfdan first saw plain, after ten years, the princess he had sped over the ice to save. And Princess

Ragnild first saw plain, after ten years, the king who had sped over the ice to save her. And each fell in love with the other.

So they were wedded.

As they sat at the bride feast, the small Prince Guthorm came up the long hall to them. He stood in front of the high seat as he had stood the first time he had come to this hall with the golden roof.

"I bring you a vow as a bride gift," he said.

"What vow is that, little brother?" asked the new Queen Ragnild.

Then said the small prince:

"When I am a man, the land of Ring-Rik will be mine. But I vow never to be its king. I give it to you, Alfdan and Ragnild, to add to your own land of Hadland."

"That is a kingly bride gift," said King Alfdan. "But why give us all you have of your own?"

"For the sake of both lands," said the small prince. "For it seems to me that when two small lands have each a king, both lands are weak. But when two small lands have the same king, both lands are strong."

Then said Torlef the Wise:

"This lad is small, but he is as wise as he is brave. This deed of his may well be the seed of a new fate for all Norway."

So the small prince dwelt with King Alfdan and Queen

Ragnild in the hall with the golden roof. So wise was he in his ways, and such skill did he show in swordcraft as he grew, that Torlef said to King Alfdan:

"As soon as he is of age to lead men, you will do well, lord, to set him over all your own men."

"This will we do," said King Alfdan, "the day he is sixteen winters old."

So time went on, till Ragnild the Golden had been a queen for three years. Then, one night, she had a dream.

In her dream, she stood in her garden. And as she stood, she felt the prick of a thorn. She felt for the thorn, and drew it forth from her dress.

As she held the thorn in her hand, it began to grow. It grew at both ends. It grew up; it grew down.

So much did it grow, so fast did it grow, that soon it had grown into a vast tree.

One end of the thorn went down among the grass. Deep, deep, deep, into the ground it went, till the tree had long, firm roots.

The other end of the thorn grew high in the air. The trunk grew thick. Far across the sky it spread long, strong twigs.

In her dream, Queen Ragnild saw that the roots of this vast tree were as red as blood. She saw that the trunk was as green as grass. She saw that the twigs were as white as snow.

She saw that so vast was the tree that from her garden it spread out over all the long land of Norway.

At dawn, Queen Ragnild told this dream to King Alfdan. King Alfdan told it to Torlef the Wise. For Torlef the Wise had much skill in dreams.

"How read you this dream, Torlef?" asked the king.

"I read it thus, lord," said Torlef. "From the queen shall spring a king who shall hold sway over all Norway."

"That will be a high fate," said King Alfdan. "But why are the roots of the tree as red as blood?"

Then said Torlef the Wise:

"Lord, I take the tree to be a son the queen will bear. And I take the blood-red roots to mean that in his first years, his root-years as king, blood will be shed to make those roots root strong and firm."

"And why a trunk as green as grass?" asked the king.

"I take the green trunk," said Torlef, "to mean that in this king's mid-years the land will be rich and bear good crops."

"And why is the top of the tree as white as snow?" asked King Alfdan.

"I take the snow-white top," said Torlef, "to mean that this king will live to be very old, with hair as white as snow."

"Why do I not dream such dreams?" asked King Alfdan.

"It may be," said Torlef, "that you do not sleep in the

48

right place for dreams. Did not the birds in his hall thatch sing to King Eric the Merry of a dream in a pigsty? When I wish to dream, I go and sleep in my pigsty."

"Then so will I," said the king.

So that night King Alfdan went to sleep in the pigsty. He lay on clean straw by the pigs. He slept. And in his sleep he had a dream.

In his dream, King Alfdan saw himself. He saw new locks of hair spring out of his head. Some grew down to his heel. Some grew to his shin. Some grew to his knee. Some grew to his hip. Some grew to his chest. Some grew to his neck. Some were but wisps that sprang out from the crown of his head.

But one lock was so long that it grew right down to the ground.

Now King Alfdan's own hair was as black as night. But in his dream, only a few of his locks were black. Some were brown. Some were red. Most of them were golden. One lock was so fair that it stood out among the rest. It was as pale as flax.

This flax-pale lock was the same lock that grew right down to the ground.

Next day at dawn, King Alfdan left the pigsty and stood at the sunrise door of his hall to greet the sun. Then he went to find Torlef the Wise. He told him his dream.

"How read you this dream in the pigsty?" he asked.

"I read it thus," said Torlef, "that from you will spring a race of kings that shall rule the land with power."

"And the long locks and the short locks?" asked King Alfdan.

"As some of the locks were long and some short," said Torlef, "so some kings shall rule with more power and some with less."

"And the fair lock so long that it grew down to the ground?" asked King Alfdan.

"As that lock is longer than the rest," said Torlef, "so shall that king rule with more power than the rest. From the queen's dream we know that he will be the first king to bring all Norway under his sway, and that he will be your son."

"I long to meet this son! May he come soon!"

And soon he came. In less than a year a son was born to King Alfdan and Queen Ragnild.

The boy was not black of hair, as his father was. Nor was he gold of hair, as his mother was. So fair was his hair that it was as pale as flax.

They gave him the name of Harald. And from his flax-pale hair he got, even as a child, the by-name of Harald Hair-Fair.

King Alfdan was thirty years old when his son was born. The boy grew into a strong child, big of frame, bold and brave, with skill in all sports. So all went well till the winter when he was ten years old and his father, King Alfdan, was forty.

When the days grew cold at the end of the fall that year, Torlef the Wise said to King Alfdan:

"Lord, take heed of the ice this winter. We gave Haki the Wolf's Head a hero's grave. This winter will show if that freed you from his death wish."

51

7: Who Stole the King's Yuletide Feast?

At the beginning of that winter, King Alfdan sent a branding iron to each farm and hall in Hadland. This was to bring the news that it was time to hold a cattle branding.

So, as soon as the ice had set on the lake, from all parts of the land men came to the Place of the Cattle Branding. And each man drove his cattle before him.

For the ten-year-old Prince Harald, this was a time of high glee. The plain of ice at the foot of Haki's grave mound was a mass of tossing backs, with wave on wave of tall white horns riding on its crest. The air was loud with new sounds — the blare of bulls, the shouts of the cowherds, the ring of hoofs on the ice.

The small prince ran in and out among the cattle. He threw ropes to help to hold them. He fed the fires with pine logs. He held branding irons in the flame to heat them. He sang songs round the fires with the cowherds.

Among the cowherds that year was a Finn. He was small and slight and dark. His name was Ross.

No other cowherd told such tales as Ross the Finn.

No other cowherd sang such songs as Ross the Finn.

Ross the Finn knew runes that were able to call up mists and snow and winds.

Ross the Finn knew runes that were able to hide the sun, and to make a bare tree seem to be in full leaf.

For in Norway in the old days it was held that all Finns were troll-wise. To be troll-wise was to have skill in witchcraft.

No other cowherd of them all was so good with cattle as Ross the Finn. He knew how to heal a cow of all her ills. With him bulls were as tame as lambs. So, when the cattle branding was over, King Alfdan kept him with him as one of his own cowherds.

And now Prince Harald spent all his time with Ross the Finn.

No more did he come to his uncle, Prince Guthorm, that he might teach him swordcraft. No more did he come to Torlef the Wise, that he might teach him booklore. No more did he come to his father, King Alfdan, that he might teach him things of state.

But he came to Ross the Finn, that he might teach

him runes, and songs, and how to skate, and how to ski.

Ross the Finn made Prince Harald snowshoes and skates of bone. They had a curl in front, like the prow of a ship. Ross the Finn spoke runes over them.

"Now they will bear you to what place you will, little prince," said Ross the Finn.

Yuletide came round. In King Alfdan's hall the long table was set for the yuletide feast. The air was full of rich steams and of rich smells. The fires were ablaze down the hall. The walls were hung with cloth-of-gold; the table was bright with the gleam of gems and of gold and of silver.

King Alfdan and Queen Ragnild sat on the high seat. Next to them sat Prince Guthorm and Torlef the Wise. But the small Prince Harald sat at the foot of the table, at the side of Ross the Finn.

And then, as the men sat down, and took up meat daggers, and put out hands to full ale horns, all in the blink of an eye, the table was as bare as a bone. Meat and drink, dish and wine cup, gem and gold and silver, all went into thin air.

"Witchcraft!" cried King Alfdan.

And from lip to lip, all down the long table, flew the cry:

"Witchcraft! Witchcraft!"

The eyes of all went to the small, dark man at the foot of the table — to the cowherd, Ross the Finn.

Then King Alfdan sent a thrall down the hall to bid Ross the Finn come to him.

Ross the Finn rose, and went up the hall, and stood in front of the high seat. The small Prince Harald rose with

55

him. He went up the hall with him. He stood in front of the high seat with him.

King Alfdan was in a black mood. His black brows drew down over his black eyes. It was clear to see that it was not only from his black hair that he had got his by-name of Alfdan the Black.

"What hand had you in this, Finn?" he cried.

"Lord, no hand at all," said Ross the Finn.

King Alfdan gave a shout of rage. "But you are troll-wise. In all this hall, Finn, only you are troll-wise. If you had no hand in it yourself, still only you can tell me who took the feast from my table."

"Lord, that is not mine to tell you," said Ross the Finn.

"That you *shall* tell me, Finn!" cried King Alfdan.

Ross the Finn stood still in front of the high seat. His eyes met the eyes of the king. He made no sound.

"Take him," said King Alfdan to his thralls. "Bind him hand and foot. Cast him into the cave room under the hall. No meat shall he have, no drink shall he have, till he tells me who took the feast from my table."

"No, Father! No, no, no!" cried the small Prince Harald.

And he tried to cling to Ross the Finn.

But King Alfdan set a strong hand on his son's arm as the thralls took Ross the Finn away.

They bound him hand and foot. They cast him

into the cave room under the hall. They shut the cave room door. They slid the bar to bolt him in.

Then twice a day King Alfdan went to the door of the cave room and asked Ross the Finn:

"Who took the feast from my table?"

And twice a day Ross the Finn told him:

"Lord, that is not mine to tell you."

On the third day, when King Alfdan had left the hall, the small Prince Harald crept to the door of the cave room, and put his mouth to its chink.

"Ross, it is I, Harald," he said in a low tone.

"Help me, little prince!" said Ross the Finn, with a gasp. "Beg the king to let me have meat and drink, or I shall die."

Prince Harald ran after King Alfdan. He cast his arms about his father's knees.

"Father, let Ross have meat and drink, I beg you," he cried. "If you do not, he will die."

"Meat and drink he shall have," said King Alfdan the Black, "when he tells me who took the feast from my table."

Then in his mind the small Prince Harald made a vow:

"Meat and drink shall my Finn have from my own hands!"

That night Prince Harald got into his bed still clad. When all was still, he rose. He stood at the door of his room

57

and held his breath and listened. Deep sleep lay on King Alfdan and on all his men.

Prince Harald crept out to the hall. The pine brands along the walls had all burnt out, but a small red glow still came from the dead fires. By that small red glow he was able to see.

Food from last night's meal lay still on the long table. Drink from last night's meal still stood on the long table. Prince Harald set a meat dagger in his belt. Full dish and full ale horn he took in his two hands.

He crept to the door of the cave room. He put his mouth to its chink.

"Ross, it is I, Harald," he said in a low tone.

He set down the dish and the ale horn, and slid back the bar that held the door fast. Into the cave room he crept.

Ross the Finn lay in the dark, bound hand and foot. The small prince felt him all over till he found his bonds. Then he drew the meat dagger from his belt and cut him free from them.

Then back he crept to the door, for the dish and the ale horn.

Ross the Finn sat up and took them. In the dark he ate and drank, and was glad and full of thanks.

"If I let you out, Ross," said Prince Harald, "can you get safe away?"

"With skates I can," said Ross the Finn.

"Skates you shall have," said the small prince. "But have you a secret place you can hide in from my father? I do not think any place in all Hadland will be safe if he stays in his black mood."

"I need not stay in Hadland," said Ross the Finn. "I can go south over the lake to King Eric the Merry in Ordland."

"Ah, that good King Eric!" said Prince Harald with a sigh. "So good, so kind, so merry, no black moods. What luck to have such a father! I wish I, too, might meet him."

"Then why not come with me to him now?" said Ross the Finn. "For it will go hard with you if you are here when the king your father finds you have set me free."

"Can a ten-year-old boy skate so far?" asked the small prince.

"Did not a ten-year-old Prince Guthorm skate from Ring-Rik to Hadland?" said Ross the Finn. "Then cannot a ten-year-old Prince Harald skate from Hadland to Ordland?"

"I will come, Ross," said Prince Harald. "Wait, while I fetch us skates and furs."

When he came back with the furs and the skates, Prince Harald said:

"Let us go out by the sunset door. That bar is less hard to lift."

They set the bar back in place on the door of the

cave room. They crept to the west door of the hall. They slid back the bar inch by inch, so that it made no sound. Inch by inch, they drew the door open. Out into the fresh night air they crept. Inch by inch, they drew the door shut.

At the edge of the lake they bound their strong skates

to their feet. Then Ross the Finn took Prince Harald's right hand in his own right hand. In his left hand he took his left.

Then, side by side, the small dark Finn and the small fair prince began to skate south by night to Ordland.

8: HOW PRINCE HARALD WENT TO KING ERIC

Over the ice, under a black sky full of sharp silver stars, sped the small Prince Harald and Ross the Finn.

The boy put up his head to sniff the fresh night air.

"The air is mild for yuletide," he said. "Will the ice hold, think you?"

"Oh yes; the wind is mild, but not so mild as to bring a thaw," said Ross the Finn. "All the same, we must take heed as we skirt the foot of Haki's grave mound."

"Why so?" asked the small Prince Harald.

"Haki's grave mound looks over the Place of the Cattle Branding," said Ross the Finn. "And it is in such a place that the thaw will set in first."

"Why so?" asked the small prince again.

"At the cattle branding, cattle dung fell on the ice," said Ross the Finn. "It eats its way into the ice; it makes it soft and weak. Ah, did you not feel the ice give then under your skate?"

"A little," said Prince Harald. "It was just here, then, that you and I first met, Ross, just under Haki's grave. Then the ice was full of men and cattle, and the air was full of the blare of bulls and the shouts of cowherds. Now only you and I are here, and the air is as still as the grave — as Haki's grave."

Ross the Finn gave a slight shiver.

"Why do you shiver?" asked the small prince. "You are not cold?"

"No," said Ross the Finn. "But you know that all Finns are a little troll-wise; and troll-wise men can see some things that are to come to pass. And when you said the air was as still as the grave, I saw that this Place of the Cattle Branding was soon to be a grave."

"So long as it is not yours or mine," said Prince Harald. "If you are troll-wise, Ross, then you knew all the time who took the yule feast from my father's table?"

"I knew, but it was not mine to tell him," said Ross the Finn.

"Can you tell me?" the small prince asked.

"You I can tell; for when next you sit at table, you will eat of that feast," said Ross. "It was King Eric the Merry."

"But why did he take it?" asked Prince Harald. "Is he so poor that he had no yule feast of his own?"

"King Eric is not rich as your father is rich," said Ross the Finn. "His hall has no golden roof. Nor is he so poor that he has need of any other king's yule feast. He took your father's feast, my prince, to draw you to him by a kind of magic after it."

"Then it is his wish that I go to him?" cried Prince Harald. "Then why did you not tell me so? And why did he not send for me?"

"If he is to help you, my prince," said Ross the Finn, "the will to go to him had to be yours."

"To help me? In what way is King Eric to help me?" asked Prince Harald.

"You have a high fate," said Ross the Finn. "But it seems it is a fate you may well let slip your mind. And King Eric can only help you to reach out to it if you come to his hall when you are ten years old."

"But how did he know I might not reach out to it?" asked Prince Harald. "He has never seen me, or I him."

"The birds that nest in his hall thatch have sung to tell him so," said Ross the Finn.

"If King Eric has such gifts," said the small prince, "why is he not rich? It seems to me he has it in his power to bend both men and things to his own ends."

"It is not his will to be rich," said Ross the Finn.

"And never will he turn his troll gifts to self-gain, but only to the good of others."

"Yet with all this," said Prince Harald, "men say no king is so merry."

"That is so," said Ross. "His is a merry hall. His red beard is awag with jests from dawn to dark."

"All his hall seems to have need of," said Prince Harald, "is a prince of my own age for me to play with."

"It has no small prince, but it has a small princess," Ross told him. "She is the same age as you; she has red hair, like her father; she is gay and high of mood; and her name is Princess Gyda."

"Oh, let us reach that hall soon!" cried Prince Harald. "How soon shall we reach it, Ross?"

"By dawn," said Ross the Finn. "By the sunset door we went out from King Alfdan's hall. By the sunrise door we will go into King Eric's."

On, on, on, as swift and as light as birds, they sped over the ice. The black sky grew less dark. The sharp stars faded.

Soon the sky began to grow pale. The forms of the trees at the edge of the lake began to grow clear.

And at last, in a gap in the line of the trees, they saw the big black bulk of a hall.

"Is that King Eric's hall?" asked Prince Harald.

"It is, my prince," said Ross the Finn. "You see, a

ten-year-old prince can skate from Hadland to Ordland!"

The sun rose as they drew near. They saw the sunrise door, the east door of the hall, swing wide. Out of it came a man, tall and big of frame. With him came a small girl. Side by side they stood at the sunrise door, to greet the sun as it rose.

"Is that King Eric?" asked Prince Harald.

"It is," said Ross the Finn.

"Is that Princess Gyda with him?" asked Prince Harald.

"It is," said Ross the Finn.

"She stands with her father to greet the sun as I stand each dawn with mine," said Prince Harald. "Ross, if my father has not yet found that I have left his hall, he will find it out now, when I do not go to greet the sun with him."

They drew in to the edge of the ice. It was mid-winter; yet as loud and sweet as if it were spring sang the birds in King Eric's hall thatch to greet the sun.

Ross the Finn bent and took off his skates. Then up the bank of the lake he went to King Eric.

Prince Harald did as the Finn did.

He saw that King Eric was big and bluff and brown of skin and red of hair and beard. He saw how his red hair and his red beard blew about him in the wind.

He saw how Princess Gyda's long red hair blew up to mix with King Eric's red beard.

"King Eric," said Ross the Finn, "I bring you Prince Harald of Hadland."

The eyes of the small prince met the eyes of the big king. Prince Harald saw that King Eric's eyes were merry.

But he saw, too, that they had the look of eyes that saw more than other eyes saw.

"If Gyda will but be true to Gyda," said King Eric, "it is not Prince Harald of Hadland that you bring me, but King Harald of Norway."

Then he bent, and took Prince Harald's small hand in his own big brown fist.

"I am glad for Norway's sake to see you, Harald Hair-Fair," he said. "So is Gyda, here, and so are the birds in my hall thatch. Gyda, take your guest in and wash his hands and feet. Give him to eat and to drink; then let him sleep. When you have slept, Harald Hair-Fair, you shall help us to eat up your father's yule feast."

Princess Gyda shook back her long red hair. She put out her hand and took the hand of Prince Harald.

She led him in by the sunrise door into King Eric's hall.

9: HOW HIS UNCLE WENT AFTER PRINCE HARALD

Just at the time when Princess Gyda led Prince Harald by the sunrise door into King Eric's hall, at the far end of the lake King Alfdan the Black went out by his own sunrise door.

Queen Ragnild and Prince Guthorm went out with him, to greet the sun. But Prince Harald was not to be seen.

"Our Hair-Fair sleeps late today," said Prince Guthorm. "I will fetch him."

For it was Prince Guthorm's way to try to shield the young prince from the black moods of King Alfdan.

Prince Guthorm was a grown man now, as brave as he was wise, and as wise as he was brave. Such was his skill in swordcraft that from the day he was sixteen years old, he had led King Alfdan's men.

In he went to Prince Harald's sleeping room. Prince Harald was not in his bed; he was not in his room; he was not in the hall.

"It may be that he went out to groom his steed," said Prince Guthorm.

And out he went to seek him in the stable.

By the dim dawn light, as he went, he saw footprints in the snow. Two sets ran side by side. He saw that they were the prints of a boy and of a man small and slight of frame.

He saw that they came from the sunset door of the hall. So he went to it, and tried it. At his light push, it swung open.

Back he went to track the footprints. From the sunset door they led down to the rim of the lake. At the edge of the ice they came to an end; but at that same spot began skate marks, two sets that ran south side by side.

They were fresh made since last sunset.

He saw that they ran to the Place of the Cattle Branding. But all the way to the foot of Haki's grave mound, the vast sheet of blue-white ice was bare. No small prince and no small slight man were to be seen on the ice.

Prince Guthorm went back and told all this to King Alfdan. King Alfdan's looks grew black.

"Two sets of skate marks?" he cried. "Find out who went with the lad!"

Prince Guthorm set his horn to his lips, and blew the note for the roll call. At the sound, his men ran and fell in, rank on rank. No gap in any rank was to be seen.

"Is the hall just as it was left last night?" asked Prince Guthorm.

His right-hand man told him:

"Lord, the table lacks one dish, one ale horn, and one meat dagger."

"Did no man wake in the night?" asked Prince Guthorm. "Did no man hear any stir in the hall?"

But no man had.

"Lord," said his right-hand man again, "well-fed men sleep deep."

"But not so men who must fast," said Prince Guthorm. "So it may be that Ross the Finn can tell us more."

He strode up the hall to the door of the cave room.

He cried in a tone that rang along the roof:

"Ross, did you hear men in the hall in the night?"

Each man in the hall held his breath. So still was it in the hall that the stir of a foot on straw was as loud as a crack of thunder. But no sound came forth from the dark cave room.

Prince Guthorm slid back the bar of the door of the cave room. He flung the door wide.

"Ross!" he cried again. "Did you hear men in the hall in the night?"

71

But still no sound came from the dark cave room. Prince Guthorm bent to stare into the gloom.

"Saxo, bring me a torch!" he said to his right-hand man.

Saxo ran to light a pine brand and to bring it to Prince Guthorm. By its red glow the prince saw the thongs that had bound Ross the Finn hand and foot. They lay, cut, on the floor. By them lay a dish, an ale horn, and a meat dagger. Save for them, the cave room was bare.

From lip to lip down the hall flew the news:

"Ross the Finn has fled! It is with Ross the Finn that our small Hair-Fair has fled!"

The eyes of King Alfdan were aflash with rage as they met the eyes of Prince Guthorm.

"So it was to steal my son from me," he cried, "that the Finn came to my hall!"

"Yet it may still be," said Prince Guthorm, "that our Hair-Fair went with him of his own free will."

"I care not if he did," cried King Alfdan the Black. "Take men, Guthorm, and track them, and bring them both back to me!"

So Guthorm and a band of the king's men set out by sledge to track the skate marks on the ice. Each sledge was drawn by three strong steeds.

Clip-clop, clip-clop, clip-clop, as swift as birds over the ice they went. On and on the tracks led them, till they came to the foot of Haki's grave mound.

Then Prince Guthorm held back his steeds, and held his hand high, to bid his men halt.

"But the tracks go on, lord," said Saxo, his right-hand man.

"They do," said Prince Guthorm. "But do you not see how soft and weak the ice is in the Place of the Cattle Branding?"

"Yet it held under the skates," said Saxo.

"Ice that holds under skate may not hold under sledge," said Prince Guthorm. "We must skirt this weak ice and pick up the skate tracks again when we are past it."

So round the edge of the weak ice went each sledge, to pick up the skate tracks again on the far side of the Place of the Cattle Branding.

Clip-clop, clip-clop, clip-clop, swift as birds on they went. On and on the tracks led them, on and on to the south end of the lake. On and on the tracks led them till they saw in a gap in the trees a tall hall with a deep thatch of straw.

"We must be on Ordland ice now," said Prince Guthorm to Saxo. "For by the straw thatch I take that to be the hall of King Eric of Ordland."

They saw that the skate marks came to an end at the rim of the lake below King Eric's hall. From the lake they saw two sets of footprints go up the snow of the bank to the sunrise door of the hall. Like the footprints that had led down to the lake from King Alfdan's sunset door, they were the prints of a boy and of a man small and slight of frame.

"So it was to King Eric the Merry that our Hair-Fair fled!" cried Saxo. "How came he to do a thing so odd and so bold?"

"This thing must go deeper than just a small lad's caper," said Prince Guthorm. "I think we shall find the hand of fate in it."

Forth from his sledge went Prince Guthorm, and up from the edge of the lake to the hall. The birds in the hall thatch sang loud as he blew a blast on the guest horn.

The door of the hall swung wide. Men came out to meet and greet him. Into the hall and up to the high seat was Prince Guthorm led with joy.

On his high seat sat King Eric, big and brown and merry. On two stools at his feet sat the small Princess Gyda and the small Prince Harald. Red head and fair head were bent over chessmen of gold and of silver. King Eric's red bush of a beard swept now fair head and now red head as he bent to help each child in turn.

That red beard shook with mirth as King Eric made jest after jest. Small prince and small princess shook with mirth under it. All the hall was loud with the mirth of King Eric's men.

It did Prince Guthorm good to see the face of the small Prince Harald so bright and gay.

But Prince Harald's bright face fell when Prince Guthorm told King Eric he had been sent to take his nephew back.

"It is not my will to go back yet, Uncle Guthorm. King Eric is a merry host; I like right well to be his guest. And Gyda is the best playmate I have ever had."

King Eric gave a merry shrug.

"If he will not go with you of his own free will, Prince Guthorm," he said, "I must not let him go at all. For he is my guest, and the guest law must be kept."

"And Ross the Finn, King Eric?"

"He, too, is my guest, and the guest law must be kept," said King Eric. "But stay this day and this night with us, and help us eat and drink King Alfdan's yule feast. At dawn you shall go back and beg King Alfdan for me to let his son stay here in Ordland till the spring."

Glad was Prince Guthorm to stay that day and that night in a hall so full of gay cheer. Long was it since he had spent a day so merry. Jest for jest he gave back to cap the jests of King Eric. Each time, the hall rang with the men's mirth. Each time, Prince Harald's face lit up. Each time, Princess Gyda shook back her long red hair to smile at him.

"Harald Hair-Fair," she said, "right well do I like your uncle, as you right well like my father. I will share my father with you, if you will share your uncle with me."

"Let us handfast that!" cried the small prince, and took her hand in his. "Now your father shall be my father, and my uncle shall be your uncle, as long as we all live."

"What if it is not my will?" asked Prince Guthorm, with a twinkle.

"Oh, but it is your will, Uncle Guthorm!" cried Princess Gyda.

"The birds in my hall thatch sing that it is fate's will," said King Eric. "Yet it still lies with a man's own will if he will do fate's will or no."

"Will our Hair-Fair, think you?"

"With Gyda to sting him on, I think he will," said King Eric. "If so, this small lad who pulls this small girl's hair will be the first king of all Norway."

"How will so vast a thing come to pass?" Prince Guthorm asked.

"So high a fate can be born only of much pain," said King Eric. "All save three small parts of Norway must be won with bloodshed."

"And those three parts?" asked Prince Guthorm.

"Hadland, Ring-Rik, and Ordland," King Eric told him. "Hadland is his by birth. Ring-Rik is his by gift — by your own gift. Ordland will be his by gift — by my own gift. But that will not be till all the rest is won."

"My gift to start, your gift to end," said Prince Guthorm.

"And all the rest the pang and clang of battle, sing my birds," King Eric said.

10: HOW HAKI'S DEATH WISH CAME TRUE

Next day, Prince Guthorm was up at dawn. With King Eric, Prince Harald, and Princess Gyda, out by the sunrise door he went to greet the sun.

Then down the snowbank to the edge of the lake they went to the sledge train. Prince Harald ran to help Saxo hold back the steeds of the first sledge as Prince Guthorm got into it. Princess Gyda ran to tuck his furs about him.

"Take care that the ice holds, Uncle Guthorm," said Prince Harald.

"Yes, Uncle Guthorm, take care that the ice holds," said Princess Gyda.

"When Ross and I came past Haki's grave mound," said the prince, "Ross saw with troll-sight that the Place of the Cattle Branding will soon be a grave."

"And not only Ross," said King Eric. "For the birds in my hall thatch sing that a breath of death steals forth from Haki's grave mound. Take care."

"Care will I take," said Prince Guthorm with a smile.

Then off over the ice went his sledge. Clip-clop, clip-clop, clip-clop, rang the hoofs of his steeds on the ice. And back to Hadland with him went his sledge train of king's men.

When Haki's grave mound came in sight, they took care to skirt the soft, weak ice in the Place of the Cattle Branding. So all came back safe and sound to the hall with the golden roof.

When Prince Guthorm came up from the lake and into the hall, King Alfdan had just begun to twist his bow a new bowstring. He saw Prince Guthorm come in, no Finn and no small prince with him. His eyebrows drew into a black frown, and so hard did he jerk the bowstring that its snap sang down the hall like a harp string.

Prince Guthorm told him how he had found the small prince with King Eric, safe and well and gay.

"And King Eric begs you will let our Hair-Fair stay with him till spring," he said.

With a face as black as a thundercloud, King Alfdan threw down his bow and strode down his hall.

"Get out my sledge!" he cried to his men. "If my son will not come when I send for him, I will go and fetch him myself."

"I beg you to let him stay, Alfdan," said Prince Guthorm. "It is good for a lad of his age to see new lands and new ways."

"You are too soft with him, Guthorm," said King Alfdan. "Fetch him back I will."

"Lord," said Torlef the Wise, "I too beg you not to go."

King Alfdan swung around on his wise man.

"You, too, Torlef?" he cried. "Are you then hand in hand with Guthorm to cross my will?"

"Lord," said Torlef, "Prince Guthorm begs you for Prince Harald's sake. I beg you for your own. Think, lord — how old are you?"

"I am forty winters old, as you well know," said King Alfdan. "But why ask of that now?"

"Forty winters old," said Torlef, "was Haki the Wolf's Head when he died on the ice. Do you not call to mind the death wish he cried on you then?"

"If you do not, Alfdan, I do," said Prince Guthorm. "This is what Haki cried in his death hour: 'You have won the Princess Ragnild, Alfdan the Black. But when you reach the age that I am now, take heed, lest the ice bring you to your death as now it brings me to mine.'"

"Of Haki in the flesh I had no fear," cried the king. "Of Haki dead I have less. Go to Ordland this day I will."

"Alfdan!" cried Queen Ragnild. "Tempt not a dead

man's death wish. Let Harald stay with King Eric till spring. Then we can all go by boat to fetch him back. Do not risk the ice when the wind is so mild it may well bring a thaw."

"No thaw has set in yet," said King Alfdan. "Go to Ordland this day I will."

And out he went, and down the snowbank to his sledge.

Prince Guthorm went with him down to the edge of the lake.

"It is true that no thaw has set in yet, Alfdan," he said. "But keep clear of the Place of the Cattle Branding. At the foot of Haki's grave mound, the ice is weak and soft; and Ross the Finn saw with troll-sight that it is soon to be a grave."

"Tell me not of the Finn!" cried King Alfdan. "Was it not he who set my son to cross my will?"

And in so red a rage did he set off that he gave no heed to what Prince Guthorm had said, but drove his steeds hard due south in a beeline for Ordland.

His whiplash sent his steeds on far ahead of the rest of the sledge train. His sledge sped on alone. And alone he came to the Place of the Cattle Branding.

So full of rage was he still that he gave no heed to the ice. He did not see, as Prince Guthorm had seen, how the cattle dung had sunk in and made the ice soft and weak. He did not see how the marks of Prince Guthorm's sledge train went round on the sound ice. He saw only that the track of the skates still went on.

And on he still went after them.

With the loud clip-clop of his steeds in his ears he did not hear the ice crack. Too late to pull up his steeds in time, he saw a black pit yawn in the blue-white ice. He felt the

sledge heel over. Down he was shot into a deep black pit of ice-cold water.

The steeds began to thrash and to rear in the water, to seek for a firm foothold. Under the ice they went. Under the ice with them they drew King Alfdan the Black.

His sledge train drew up at the edge of the Place of the Cattle Branding. Each man left his sledge and crept on hands and knees to the rim of the black pit.

"I will go in after him," said Saxo. "Tie a lifeline to my belt, and pull in hard when I tug it."

To Saxo's belt they tied a lifeline, and held it tight. Into the water he went, and they saw the deep black water close over his head.

They felt him tug. They drew the lifeline in. When he came up, he had King Alfdan limp in his arms. They took the dead king from him. They drew Saxo onto the ice.

Back to the sledge train at the foot of Haki's grave mound they bore the dead king. Back they bore Saxo, limp but still alive. Back sped the sledge train to the hall with the golden roof.

Sad and slow rang the steps of the men as they bore the dead king up the long hall, and laid him at the feet of Queen Ragnild.

Queen Ragnild knelt and wept over him as with white hands she made smooth his wet black hair. But Torlef the Wise stood with grave face and bit his lip, his hand on his beard, for he saw the rocks and the reefs that lay ahead.

He said to Prince Guthorm:

"Come back now Prince Harald must. But your place is with the queen; she will need you in her loss. So this time it is I who must go and bring our small king home."

So over the ice sped the sledge train again to Ordland.

As it drew in at the rim of the lake, Torlef the Wise saw King Eric come to the door of his hall. As still as a stout brown tree he stood in the snow, to catch the drift of the song the birds sang so loud in his hall thatch.

Up the snowbank to him came Torlef. He told him all that had come to pass.

"Your Hair-Fair and my Gyda went up to the hills, to ski with Ross the Finn," King Eric said. "I will send men to bring him to you. And now, come in and eat."

As they sat at meat, Torlef said:

"See how the ill wish Haki cried in his death hour the king's own rage has made come true! And see now the ill fate it brings for Hadland and for Ring-Rik! For a strong king has died in his prime and has left his two lands to a lad but ten years old!"

"Yet with you and Queen Ragnild and Prince Guthorm to teach him how to rule," said King Eric, "even so small a lad can be a strong king too."

"It is the king's men, lord, who will not wish to take so small a lad for king," said Torlef. "If Prince Guthorm will take it, the crown of both lands is his."

King Eric sat with his big red beard in his big brown fist.

"I think that may be his men's will, but not his," said King Eric. "For it is his own dream to help the dream in the pigsty to come true. And Harold Hair-Fair must needs first be king of his own two small lands if he is to end as king of all Norway."

"Think you he will so end?" asked Torlef.

"It was a fate he might well have let slip his mind," said King Eric, "had he not met my Gyda. But my child has red hair, Torlef; she will sting him to reach out to what fate wills for him if he will but will it, too. To that end I made my plans for them to meet this yuletide. That, Torlef, is why you now eat of King Alfdan's yuletide feast."

Then Torlef saw Ross the Finn come into the hall.

And with him, hand in hand, eyes bright and cheeks aglow, came the small Prince Harald and the small Princess Gyda.

Then Torlef told Prince Harald of his father's death.

Prince Harald laid his small hand in the big fist of King Eric.

"I must go back to my mother; she will need me," he said.

Then he threw out his arms and gave Gyda a big hug.

"Never will I forget you, Gyda," he said. "See that

84

you do not forget me. For as soon as I am of age to wed, I shall send for you to come and be my bride."

Gyda gave a toss of her red head.

"The man I wed," said she, "must be king of more than two small lands!"

"What then must he be king of?" asked Prince Harald.

"All Norway," said the princess.

"Then that will I be!" said the prince.

Then back he went with Torlef to the hall with the golden roof.

11: HOW THE DREAM IN THE PIGSTY CAME TRUE

Glad was Queen Ragnild when her son came home. Glad, too, was his uncle, Prince Guthorm. But the king's men stood back, and gave the lad cold looks.

"Be honest with me, Prince Guthorm," said Torlef the Wise. "If your men so will, is it your will to take the crown?"

"My will it is not," said Prince Guthorm. "And if it is my men's will, such it shall not be for long."

That night, as his men lay down to sleep, he said to them:

"The day will soon be set when we shall take Prince Harald as our king. Let each of you rub his helmet and shield and coat of mail bright, to match the new gold arm rings he will give you on that day."

He saw how each man's face grew dark at this. Each man began to growl in his beard.

"A lad ten winters old is no king for us, lord," said Saxo.

Said the next man:

"We need a grown man for king, wise in the ways of war, lord, and with skill in swordcraft."

Then all the men gave a shout:

"We need you, lord! It is our will, Prince Guthorm, to take you for our king!"

Prince Guthorm's eyes went from face to face. His own face was stern. He stood still, and did not speak.

"Lord, the land of Ring-Rik is your land by right," cried Saxo. "When your father, King Sigurd the Hart, was slain, you were as small a lad as Prince Harald is now. So you did not take it then. Now the time is ripe for you to do so."

"Men!" cried Prince Guthorm then. "All of you sat in this hall when Ragnild my sister wedded King Alfdan. Do you call to mind what I said then? If you cannot tell me, I will tell you."

Then Saxo said:

"Lord, you said this: 'I bring a vow as a bride gift. The land of Ring-Rik is mine, but I vow never to be its king. I give it to you, Alfdan and Ragnild, to add to your own land of Hadland. For it seems to me that when two small lands have each a king, both lands are weak. But when two small lands have the same king, both lands are strong.'"

"That vow I have kept," said Prince Guthorm. "That vow I will still keep. Take our Hair-Fair as king of both lands, and you will find he has a high fate in store. As for the lad's age, that is a thing time will soon cure."

"And till then, lord?" asked Saxo.

And Prince Guthorm told the men:

"Till then, Queen Ragnild and Lord Torlef will rule for him in things of state and teach him statecraft. I will lead his men as I led his father's; and we, his men, will teach him swordcraft and the ways of war. Men, I think that out of this small lad we shall make a strong king!"

At that, a cheer went up from the men.

"On such terms, lord," they cried, "we will take our Hair-Fair as king!"

So, on the day set by Torlef, the small Prince Harald sat in his father's big high seat. And one by one his men came up the long hall to him, and put a big hand in his small ones, and took him to be king.

Bright was the hall with cloth-of-gold that day. Bright was each helmet, each shield, each coat of mail. Bright were the gold arm rings the new king gave his men that day.

Rich was the feast that night. Long sat the men at the long table, and ate and drank and made merry.

Now the slow years went by, and King Harald Hair-Fair grew up.

All went well all this time with his two small lands of Hadland and Ring-Rik. Yet it was no thanks to him that this was so, for he left it to others to rule them. Nor did he show any wish to add other lands to his own.

As time went on in this way, his men said to each other:

"Is this the strong king, wise in the ways of war, we were to have had? This is no king, but a milksop who moons in the hall from dawn to dusk."

And Queen Ragnild said to herself with a sigh:

"When will this small thorn, that my son is still, grow into the vast tree of my dream?"

And even Torlef the Wise shook his head, and said to Prince Guthorm:

"Was not Harald Hair-Fair born to do more than this, to be more than this? The years go by, yet he lifts no hand to make the dream in the pigsty come true!"

"Put your trust in King Eric, Torlef," said Prince Guthorm. "Did he not say Princess Gyda had stung our Hair-Fair to stretch out his hand to his fate? We shall yet see that in due time this he will do."

So the time came when King Harald was of age to wed.

He sent for his uncle, Prince Guthorm. He sent for his wise man, Torlef. He told them:

"When I was ten winters old, I chose Princess Gyda of Ordland to be my bride. Go now to her father, King Eric, and ask her hand of him for me."

Prince Guthorm and Torlef the Wise took a band of the king's men. They took a ship with red ropes and with sails of blue and white silk. And in this they went south down the lake to the hall of King Eric of Ordland.

King Eric was still big and stout and brown and merry. His red head and his red beard had still not one white hair.

When they told him why they came, his red beard began to wag with mirth.

"He sent you to ask her hand of *me*?" he cried. "Never tell Gyda that! Her hair is red, as you well know, and she is apt to flare up as a pine brand! She is a maid with a mind of her own, a maid with a will of her own. Let us find that mind out now."

He led them up the stone stairs that went from the hall to her bower.

In her bower, Princess Gyda sat at a silver loom, and wove bright cloth-of-gold. Her hair, as she bent to the loom, was like a wave of flame.

Her silver shuttle flew to and fro. From edge to edge of the cloth it drew the gold thread with a flash like that of a spear.

She rose as they came in, and they saw that she was

90

as tall and as swift and as strong as a spear herself.

"Uncle Guthorm!" she cried.

And she came to him and took both his hands in hers.

"Is it to see my father or is it to see me that you come after so many years?" she asked.

Just in time, Prince Guthorm saw the twinkle in King Eric's eye.

"To see you, Gyda," he said. "Do you call to mind how, when you were ten years old, Harald Hair-Fair told you of his wish to wed you? Now you are both of age to wed, and he sends me to ask you if you will now be his bride."

She threw up her bright head and shook her red hair back in just her old way as a child.

"You were not with us, Uncle Guthorm," she said, "but Lord Torlef was. So he knows, if you do not, that I told Harald Hair-Fair then not to send for me till he had put all Norway under him. Now both of you go back, and tell him that again."

"But stay and eat first," said the merry King Eric.

As the three sat at meat, he said:

"My red Gyda has the fire that Harald Hair-Fair lacks. Sure fire he needs if he is to reach out to grasp his fate. Tell him from me that when he has won the rest of Norway, Ordland shall be his as my bride-gift."

So, in the ship with red ropes and with blue and white silk sails, Prince Guthorm and Torlef the Wise went north

91

up the lake to the hall with the golden roof.

"Think you he will flare into red rage when we tell him?" Torlef asked Prince Guthorm. "Or fall into a black mood, like his father?"

"I do not know," said Prince Guthorm. "He is my own sister's son; yet I feel that much must lie deep in him that I have not yet seen."

So they came to King Harald and told him:

"Princess Gyda bids us tell you she will not wed you till you have put all Norway under you."

King Harald did not flare into red rage. Nor did he fall into a black mood, like his father. He sat still for a time on his high seat, his flax-pale head on his hand. Then he said:

"I owe Gyda thanks. For she brings to my mind things I need to think of. Here and now I make this vow: That I will not clip nor cut my hair till I have put all the land of Norway under me."

Then was Torlef glad that Gyda had stung Harald to reach out to grasp his high fate. And glad was Queen Ragnild to see the small thorn of her dream start to grow at last. And Prince Guthorm cried, for his own self and for all the king's men:

"Harald, it is with joy we hear you vow a vow so kingly!"

From that day King Harald Hair-Fair let his fair hair grow. He did not clip it; he did not cut it.

So fast it grew, so long it grew, that the time came when his flax-pale locks were as long as Gyda's red ones. So fast it grew, so long it grew, that the time came when his flax-pale locks were as long as the long fair lock in King Alfdan's dream.

And now just to see this man with the long pale hair at the head of his men struck fear into his foes. For as his hair grew in length, so did he grow in strength, and in skill, and in wisdom. He grew wise in the ways of men and of wars; he grew in skill in swordcraft and statecraft; he grew into a strong king.

With Prince Guthorm he led out the men of Hadland and Ring-Rik to win land after land. In battle after battle the swords sang and the spears thundered. In battle after battle coats of mail were cleft and shields were bent and helmets rent, and blades grew hot, and fields grew red.

As in Queen Ragnild's dream, the roots of the tree that was King Harald were roots as red as blood.

And many, many were the roots that had to be torn up that King Harald's might be firm and strong. Many kings and many king's men fell in battle. Many came to King Harald, to be his men. Many who held still to the old ways had to flee from Norway, to hew out a new life in new lands. Others fled to sea, and, as Vikings, set sail in long ships to rob and to raid other lands.

After three years, King Harald Hair-Fair was the only free king save one left in all Norway. The other free king was King Eric the Merry of Ordland.

Then back to his hall with its golden roof came King Harald Hair-Fair. He cut his long locks short. He sent for Prince Guthorm and Torlef the Wise.

"To them he said:

"Now go again to Princess Gyda. Tell her that now I have all Norway under me."

So again Prince Guthorm and Torlef took a band of the king's men. Again they took a ship with red ropes and sails of blue and white silk. And in it again they went south down the lake to the hall of King Eric of Ordland.

Gladly, then, did Princess Gyda go back with them, her hair like locks of flame. Gladly, too, went King Eric, big and stout and brown and merry, his red beard blown this way and that as he stood in the prow of the ship.

Gladly did King Harald and Queen Ragnild meet them. Glad and rich and merry was the bride feast. And gladly did King Eric keep his vow, and give to King Harald his own small land of Ordland as a bride-gift.

And now began the long, long years of joy and plenty, the years that in Queen Ragnild's dream were the trunk of the tree as green as grass. Now all the land of Norway was at rest. The crops grew ripe. The barns were full.

When at last King Harald Hair-Fair died, he was eighty-three years old. His flax-pale locks had for many years been as white as snow, as white as the twigs on the tree in Queen Ragnild's dream.

In this wise did Harald Hair-Fair come to be the first king to hold sway over all Norway.

And in this wise did Queen Ragnild's dream and the dream in the pigsty come true.